D0604051

Heidi

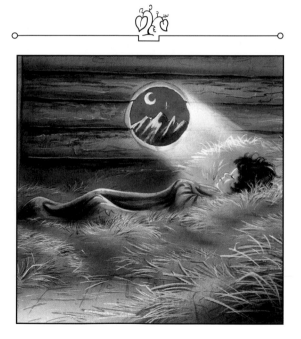

In the heart of the Swiss Alps, in a charming cottage, lived a girl named Heidi. After her parents died, her grandfather welcomed her into his home and they lived a quiet life together. Her best friend was a young goatherd named Peter.

Every day, Heidi joined Peter when he took his goats out to pasture.

"How I love the mountains!" Heidi often said as she looked out at the peaks. She liked picking flowers and making beautiful bouquets to cheer up her grandfather's home.

"Heidi, you fill my days with sunshine," said her grandfather with a smile.

Heidi waited for winter impatiently. It was her favorite season! As soon as there was enough snow, Heidi and her grandfather slid down the mountain on their sled to go to the village for supplies.

"Faster, Grandpa! Faster !" cried Heidi. Their laughter caused the animals to race out of the way of the speeding sled.

One spring, Heidi's aunt arrived.
She wanted to take Heidi to Frankfurt to
keep a girl named Klara company. Klara
was ill and spent her days in a wheelchair.

Heidi was very unhappy to be leaving her
grandfather, Peter, and the beautiful
mountains. She waved goodbye for a long
time as she rode away.

Klara was a small blonde girl with pale skin. In no time, she and Heidi became friends. They loved to play together. Every morning, a teacher came to the house to give the girls their lessons. Heidi and Klara studied very hard.

Sometimes, in the afternoon, Heidi took a walk through the town to the church.

She climbed all the way up to the bell
tower because it was the only place where
she could catch a glimpse of her beloved
mountains in the distance.

"How I miss you," she sighed.

One day, during her walk, Heidi found some abandoned kittens. "I'm sure these little kittens will make Klara so very happy!" Heidi thought to herself as she took them home with her.

"Oh Heidi! They are just adorable!" said Klara. Heidi was delighted that her friend was pleased.

Their teacher, however, was far from pleased. The lively kittens got into all kinds of trouble and kept the girls from concentrating on their lessons. One morning, one of the kittens overturned the inkwell and then jumped onto the teacher's pant leg. He was furious, but Klara and Heidi couldn't help but giggle at the sight.

That summer, Heidi was allowed to return to her grandfather's home. She would finally see the mountains once again!

"Klara, why don't you come with me?"
Heidi asked.

Klara's family agreed, deciding the fresh
air would do her good.

"Heidi, my dear!" said Grandfather,
holding her tight, when she arrived.

Klara met Peter and his goats, which were
very affectionate with the newcomer.

In a matter of days, thanks to the invigorating mountain air and the fresh goat's milk, Klara started looking healthier and stronger. Heidi had never seen her smile so much.

One morning when Peter went to visit his friends, he nudged Klara's wheelchair and it rolled down the hill. He wasn't able to stop it before it crashed into some boulders. Peter felt terrible. How would Klara get around now!

"I guess I'll just have to walk!" Klara said. With Heidi and Peter's help, she took a few steps just as her father arrived at the mountaintop.

"It's a miracle!" he cried.

Thanks to the fresh mountain air, friendship and her determination, Klara was able to overcome her illness.